FRIENDS
OF ACPL

J
DICKS,
SALLY ANN ON HER OWN

W9-BBD-734

DO NOT REMOVE
CARDS FROM POCKET

ALLEN COUNTY PUBLIC LIBRARY

FORT WAYNE, INDIANA 46802

You may return this book to any agency, branch,
or bookmobile of the Allen County Public Library.

8/92

DEMCO

Sally Ann on Her Own

Sally Ann on Her Own

By TERRANCE DICKS

Illustrated by
BLANCHE SIMS

SIMON & SCHUSTER BOOKS FOR YOUNG READERS
Published by Simon & Schuster
New York • London • Toronto • Sydney • Tokyo • Singapore

Allen County Public Library
Ft. Wayne, Indiana

 SIMON & SCHUSTER BOOKS FOR YOUNG READERS
Simon & Schuster Building, Rockefeller Center
1230 Avenue of the Americas, New York, New York 10020
Text Copyright © 1987 by Terrance Dicks
Illustrations Copyright © 1992 by Blanche Sims
All rights reserved
including the right of reproduction
in whole or in part in any form.
Originally published in Great Britain by Piccadilly Press Ltd.
SIMON & SCHUSTER BOOKS FOR YOUNG READERS
is a trademark of Simon & Schuster.

Designed by Lucille Chomowicz
Manufactured in the United States of America
10 9 8 7 6 5 4 3 2 1

Library of Congress Cataloging-in-Publication Data
Dicks, Terrance.
Sally Ann on her own / Terrance Dicks : illustrated by Blanche Sims.
p.   cm.
Summary: Sally Ann the doll, one of the toys in a day care center, is instrumental in saving
the building from the clutches of two greedy crooks.
ISBN 0-671-74512-3
[1. Dolls—Fiction.   2. Toys—Fiction.   3. Day care centers—Fiction.]
I. Sims, Blanche.   II. Title.
PZ7.D5627Sal   1991
[E]—dc20   91-15379 CIP AC

ISBN: 0-671-74512-3

Contents

Sally Ann on Her Own

1
Sally Ann Arrives

"And this is Sally Ann," said the visitor. "She used to belong to my daughter Jenny, till Jenny got too big for dolls. She lived on the shelf in my son Jimmy's room with his toys for a while. But I think he was a bit embarrassed to have a doll there. So when I heard you were asking for toys for your day care center . . ."

"It really is most kind of you," said Mrs. Foster, the day care lady. "I'll just pop her in the toy closet with the others. I'm sure the children will love her."

Sally Ann was lifted out of the plastic bag she'd been brought in. She was set down on a broad shelf in a closet. The door was slammed shut, and she was left in darkness. She could sense the shapes of other toys around her.

Sally Ann was a doll of decision, and she liked to know what was going on.

Lifting her foot, she booted the door from the inside so that it creaked slowly open.

Mrs. Foster looked up. "Oh, dear, that door's always opening. I'll have to get someone in to fix it someday!"

The two women went on chatting while Sally Ann took the opportunity to

look around. She was excited and worried at the same time. Life on Jimmy's shelf had been boring sometimes. But would this be any better? The toy closet was in the far corner of a big, comfortable room, with windows that looked out on an overgrown yard.

Once it had been a family's living room. There were still comfortable, squashy armchairs and sofas covered in flowery material.

But now there were lots of other things in it too.

There was a story corner, with floor cushions and lots of picture books in a special rack.

There was an activity corner, with big wooden tables, where you could paint, and cut things out, and make things. And a plastic carpet so it didn't matter if something spilled.

There was a playhouse and climbing bars and a game cabinet, an old piano, a record player, and a TV set.

Almost everything you could think of to keep children entertained and amused.

After looking around the room, Sally Ann looked at her companions. She was pleased to see a number of different toys on the shelf with her.

A big, shabby gray velvet elephant.

A very fat teddy bear.

A skinny monkey in a red satin vest. He had a mischievous face. He was holding a drum and two little sticks.

There was a long, wriggly green velvet python with black button eyes.

And finally there was a very pretty doll with a frilly dress, long golden hair, and big blue eyes with long eyelashes.

There were other toys too, but Sally Ann couldn't see them from where she was sitting. She didn't want to break the rules by moving when humans might see her—not yet anyway.

So she started looking at, and listening to, the two women who were still chatting over their coffee and cake.

The woman who'd brought her was saying, "I'm so sorry you're having such a struggle, Mrs. Foster. I thought you were doing really well."

Mrs. Foster was a plump, kind-looking lady with straggly brown hair that was just beginning to turn gray.

She tried to wear it on top of her head in a bun, but the bun was always coming undone. She left a trail of hairpins behind her.

She wore big round glasses, which she hung around her neck on a silver chain because she was always losing them.

"I do have quite a lot of customers," said Mrs. Foster. "You see, lots of mothers around here have to work. They need somewhere to leave the children while they're out. There's the after-school club for bigger ones too. They come after school and stay till their mothers and fathers get home from work."

She sighed. "But this is such a big old house to look after, and there are heating bills and electric bills. And, of course, my helpers have to be paid. Somehow whatever I earn seems to be just a bit less than what I need."

"Maybe you should charge more money," suggested her visitor.

Mrs. Foster looked shocked. "Oh, I couldn't do that. Most of my mothers can only just manage themselves. They can afford to bring their children here only because I charge a bit less than most places. If I raise my fees, they couldn't come at all."

She sighed again, a bigger noise this time. "We always just about managed, though, or we did till those two men came around. . . ."

She went on talking, and Sally Ann listened in horror. It looked as if she might lose her new home before she'd really arrived.

Later that evening, when the two ladies had gone and everything was quiet, all the toys came to life.

Toys always do when there aren't any people around. But the rules say they mustn't do it when anyone might see them.

"Wakey, wakey, everybody!" Jacko the monkey did a little roll on his drum to wake everyone up. Then he introduced Sally Ann to her new companions.

The gray velvet elephant was named Clarence. He gave Sally Ann his trunk to shake. "Hope you like it here," he said sadly. Clarence said everything sadly. "It's not too bad, I suppose."

The fat teddy bear was named Arthur. "Oh, don't be such an old misery, Clarence," he said in a fat, jolly voice. "It's great here, and you know it."

The green snake was called Kaa. "Yess," he hissed. "It'sss absssolutely ssuper!" He was a very posh python.

The pretty doll was called Stella. She fluttered her eyelashes disapprovingly at Sally Ann. "I really don't think you should have broken the rules like that. Somebody might have seen you kick that closet door."

"Nonsense," said Sally Ann briskly. "They wouldn't have believed their eyes if they had seen me. You heard them explain it away."

"But rules are rules. . . ."

"And rules are made to be broken — some rules sometimes anyway!"

Stella looked shocked.

Sally Ann jumped down from her shelf and stood, hands on hips, looking up at her companions.

"I'm very pleased to meet you all," she began. "My name's Sally Ann."

Jacko jumped down beside her. "You haven't met us all yet, only the toys on our shelf."

"We'll make the rest of the introductions later," said Sally Ann. "Right now you've all got to listen to me. This whole place is in terrible danger. Unless we do something, it's going to close down. And we'll all be stuck at the bottoms of toy closets for the rest of our lives!"

2
Sally Ann Makes a Plan

The toys stared at her in horror.

Stella said slowly, "But that means we'll all just . . . fade away."

They all knew what she meant.

Toys take their lives from the humans they live with. All toys need to be loved and cared for and played with fairly regularly. If they're not . . .

"We wouldn't be able to come to life

at all," groaned Clarence. "Even when humans aren't around . . ."

"Well, we're not going to let it happen," said Sally Ann fiercely. "We must do something!"

"*Do* sssomething?" hissed Kaa.

"What can we do?" asked Arthur. "We're only toys."

"I'm only a doll." Stella sighed. "What can I do?"

Sally Ann glared at them. "Don't be so wimpy. You can always do something. At least, you can always try."

"Sally Ann's right," said Jacko. He gave a little roll on his drum. "What we must do is . . ." He looked at Sally Ann. "What must we do, Sally Ann?"

"Yesss," hissed Kaa. "Tell usss!"

"Tell us, Sally Ann!" chorused the rest of the toys.

Things like this were always happening to Sally Ann.

She was a born leader.

Sally Ann thought hard. "The first thing we must do is find out more about what's going on."

"How do we do that?" asked Arthur.

"We listen. The humans will talk about it, they always do. If all of us keep our ears open, we should be able to get the whole story."

"Fat chance of hearing anything in all that racket," grumbled Clarence. "When the humans are back, the center will be open. You don't know what you're in for, Sally Ann!"

Sally Ann saw what he meant the very next morning.

After breakfast Mrs. Foster and her

two part-time helpers came around checking that everything was ready.

Then the children started arriving, brought in by harassed and hurried parents on their way to work.

Soon the children were swarming all over the playroom. Children of every shape and size were painting and draw-

ing and listening to stories, swinging on the climbing bars, and rushing in and out of the playhouse. And, of course, playing with the toys.

Sally Ann was grabbed by a chubby little girl in a jump suit. She had made straight for the toy closet and spotted the new arrival right away.

"New dolly," she shouted. "Mine!"

She grabbed Sally Ann in a bear hug.

Mrs. Foster smiled. "That's Sally Ann, Lucy, she came to us yesterday. You can play with her for a while, but later you must share her with the others."

Mrs. Foster was strong on sharing.

Lucy wasn't. "My dolly," she roared. "Mine, mine, *mine*!"

Mrs. Foster smiled. Lucy was the youngest child in the day care center. She was at the age some people call the terrible twos. "We'll see," she said soothingly. "Why don't you go and show Sally Ann to your friends?"

Lucy trotted off. She hung on to Sally Ann fiercely, but before too long she decided she wanted to do some painting. She "lended" Sally Ann to someone else.

The busy day seemed to go by very quickly.

Later the bigger children arrived, the ones in the after-school club.

Things quieted down then. The toddlers had worn themselves out, and some of them took naps on the big soft cushions. The bigger children settled down to reading or watching television.

Very soon Mrs. Foster and her helpers
served snacks.

There were sandwiches and apples
and cookies and lemonade, and coffee
for the grown-ups.

Not too long after that the parents started to arrive, picking up their children on their way home from work.

The bigger children went home by themselves. Suddenly the place was quiet again.

Mrs. Foster and her helpers went off for a well-earned rest. Once again the toys were on their own.

Sally Ann jumped down from the shelf and looked around. "Okay, what did we find out?"

All the toys started to talk at once. "One at a time!"

"It started when these two men came around," began Arthur.

"Mrs. Foster thought everything was all right, but they told her she was breaking all kinds of new rules about day care centers," said Clarence mournfully.

"She would have to sspend lotsss and lotsss of money to put thingsss right," hissed Kaa.

"That's more or less what I heard when little Lucy finally let me out of the playhouse," said Sally Ann.

Mrs. Foster had talked about her problems with the helpers and with the parents who brought and picked up the children. Between them the toys had overheard quite a lot.

"But didn't we learn anything new?" Sally Ann asked.

"I heard something about a letter," whispered Stella.

"Out with it," ordered Sally Ann. "It could be important."

Stella had a hard time remembering what she'd heard. But they kept asking questions and eventually got it out of her.

The day after the two men had arrived, Mrs. Foster had a letter offering to buy the house. It wasn't a very good offer, but there would be just enough money to pay all her debts and a little left over.

The bad news was that she was thinking of taking it.

"She said she was so worried she didn't know where to turn," said Stella sadly. "She said she'd just have to sell the house and go away."

There was a shocked silence.

"She can't," said Sally Ann fiercely. "We won't let her."

Even Jacko was depressed. "What else can she do? If things are as bad as they seem . . ."

"Things are never as bad as they seem," said Sally Ann. She stood up. "There's only one thing to do. I'm going to have to talk to her!"

There was a chorus of dismay from all the toys. "You can't, Sally Ann. It's against all the rules to talk to humans," protested Clarence.

"Yess, it is mosst sstrictly forbidden," hissed Kaa.

"You let me worry about that," said Sally Ann. "This is an emergency. I'm going to talk to her tonight!"

The toys tried to talk her out of it,

but, as usual, Sally Ann had her own way.

In the middle of the night, when the big old house was quiet and still, she slipped out of the playroom closet. Sally Ann soon started climbing the stairs toward Mrs. Foster's bedroom.

3

Sally Ann in Action

Mrs. Foster wasn't really asleep.

She was dozing and dreaming and worrying about her problems at the same time.

She hated the idea of losing the day care center.

She'd started it after her husband had died, to keep herself busy and to earn enough money to keep her big old house.

Although she had never had children of her own, she loved looking after other people's. And the parents had become her friends. What would they say when she told them she was closing down?

Although some of the time she was awake and worrying, some of the time she was asleep and dreaming.

Suddenly she felt a tap on her foot and a voice whispered, "Wake up, wake up! I've got to talk to you!"

Mrs. Foster opened her eyes and reached for her glasses. Peering sleepily around her, she saw Sally Ann sitting on the end of the bed. "Oh, hello, Sally Ann, what are you doing here?" She was too tired to be surprised.

"I've got to talk to you," repeated Sally Ann. "We've got to find a way to save your day care center."

Mrs. Foster leaned over and switched on her bedside light, still a bit dazed. "How can we? These men said—"

"What men? Who were they? Where did they come from?"

"From town hall, I suppose. They said new regulations had been passed about day care centers. I know that's true, I read it in the papers. They said unless I made all sorts of improvements, I'd have to close down."

Sally Ann frowned. "Did they show you any identification?"

"Well, no, but they were very official-looking. They had dark suits and briefcases and neckties."

"Anyone can buy those. Did they tell you their names?"

"Mr. Perkins and Mr. Peck."

"And you didn't check up on them?"

"No, I didn't think. They left me a phone number, though."

Sally Ann sighed. Some humans were hopeless. "When you first started the center, didn't you see someone about all the rules and regulations?"

"Yes, the social services adviser. A nice young woman named Molly Morris."

Sally Ann thought very hard. "And the day after the men were here the letter came offering to buy the house?"

"Yes, from a real estate office called Tinpot and Tring."

Sally Ann was thinking furiously. "Sounds suspicious to me. Look, do you know any policemen?"

"Only Officer Craddock. He looks after the crossing outside the center sometimes."

"Right," said Sally Ann. "Now, here's what you've got to do. . . ."

She gave Mrs. Foster her instructions, who to call and when and what to say.

Then she told her all over again.

Then she made Mrs. Foster go over them a third time to make sure she'd got it right.

"I've got it, I've got it," said Mrs. Foster at last. "Now I must get some sleep."

She turned out her light and settled down. "Good night, Sally Ann."

"Good night," said Sally Ann.

She jumped off the bed and made her way downstairs.

As she slowly drifted off to sleep, it occurred to Mrs. Foster that it was rather strange being told how to solve her problems by a bossy rag doll called Sally Ann.

Then she smiled.

It was obvious. The whole thing was just a dream. . . .

When she got back to the playroom, Sally Ann's new friends crowded around.

"Did you really do it?" asked Arthur. "You talked to a human?"

"Yes, of course I did. Humans are nothing to be scared of. They're not nearly as sensible as most toys. Poor Mrs. Foster didn't have the slightest idea what to do next. But I told her!"

"She musst have been asstonished, ssurely?" hissed Kaa.

"Not really. I imagine she thought she was dreaming. Humans are very good at making up explanations for themselves."

"I don't know how you dared, Sally Ann," said Stella.

And Clarence the elephant grumbled, "If she thinks it's all a dream, then you've been wasting your time. She'll forget all about it in the morning."

"Oh, no, she won't," said Sally Ann. "Not the way I drummed it into her."

Jacko drummed softly on his little drum. "That's the way, Sally Ann. Drum it in!"

All the other toys in the closet crowded around, demanding to know what was going on.

An old stuffed lion named Albert was very severe, saying Sally Ann had gone too far.

But a wise old owl named Mortimer said she was right. "Sally Ann is an example to us all."

The toys argued among themselves for the rest of the night. When dawn came, they fell silent, sleeping on their shelves. Only Sally Ann stayed awake.

Was Clarence right? she wondered. Would Mrs. Foster forget everything in the morning? Decide it was all a silly dream and take no notice?

At any rate, decided Sally Ann, she'd tried. In the end that was all anyone could do.

Now she'd just have to wait and see what happened.

It would be terrible if the center closed down and she lost her new home and all her new friends.

Sally Ann had done all she could.

Now it was up to Mrs. Foster.

Sally Ann sighed.

The trouble with humans, especially

grown-up ones, was that they were so scatterbrained and unreliable.

And if Mrs. Foster forgot her instructions, the center was doomed.

Sally Ann made up her mind to be hopeful. Mrs. Foster just had to remember. She *had* to.

4

"Remember the Plan!"

Mrs. Foster overslept.

She got up late and had to rush around getting washed and dressed and preparing the center for opening time. She had no time for breakfast. She was only just ready by the time the first of the parents arrived. She was flustered all morning.

Somehow nothing went right.

All the good children were bad and the bad ones were just awful. Paint was spilled and a glass was broken during morning snack. It took Mrs. Foster most of the morning to get things running normally. It was ages before she had time to sit down for a cup of coffee and a cookie.

Sally Ann was watching her in despair.

You could tell just by looking at her that Mrs. Foster was in no state to remember anything, certainly not a fairly complicated plan.

It was time for desperate measures, decided Sally Ann.

She was still in Lucy's clutches at the time. The determined two-year-old had reclaimed her favorite doll.

Sally Ann came to life.

She wriggled around and whispered
in Lucy's ear.

"Let's go and see Mrs. Foster, Lucy.
She's having a cup of coffee over there in
the corner!"

Lucy had lined up a little group of toys for the tenth time, and was playing house.

"Don't wanna," she said. "Wanna stay here."

Sally Ann wasn't standing for any nonsense.

"Lucy," she said in her sternest voice, "you take me over to see Mrs. Foster *right now*!"

Lucy gave her an astonished look, then picked her up and trotted over to Mrs. Foster.

She held up the rag doll. "Sally Ann wants you!"

Mrs. Foster gave a tired smile. "And what does she want?"

"She wants *you*!" repeated Lucy. "She talked!"

Mrs. Foster looked at Sally Ann and smiled. What wonderful imaginations little children had.

Sally Ann leaned forward and said fiercely, "The plan. Remember the plan!"

"See," said Lucy. "I told you she talked."

Dropping Sally Ann on Mrs. Foster's lap, she ran off to play, not at all surprised.

Mrs. Foster stared at Sally Ann and suddenly she thought of her dream. Only perhaps it wasn't a dream after all.

"Yes, of course, the plan!" she said.

Taking Sally Ann with her, she went over to the phone in the corner.

Mrs. Foster was showing Molly Morris,

the social services adviser, around the day care center. It was nearly the end of the afternoon.

If Molly was surprised to see Sally Ann tucked under Mrs. Foster's arm, she was too polite to say anything.

When they'd finished, Molly, who was a cheerful, plump young woman with little round glasses, said, "There's nothing wrong at all! You're obeying *all* the rules. I told you that when you opened. You ought to have a new fire-guard around that old radiator, but that won't cost more than a few dollars. And I've never heard of these Perkins and Peck people. They're certainly not in my department!"

From under Mrs. Foster's arm Sally Ann whispered. "Call them. And ask her to stay!"

Molly looked puzzled. "I'm sorry, did you say something?"

"I wonder if you could stay a little longer?" asked Mrs. Foster. "I think I'll call them and try to clear things up!"

"Wouldn't miss it for anything," said Molly. "I'll go and help with the kids while you're calling."

Mrs. Foster called the number the two men had given her. "Mr. Perkins? Oh, it's Mr. Peck! Could you come by right away please and go over all those rules I'm breaking? I'm thinking of selling the house, you see. I've just had an offer, but I want to be sure I'm doing the right thing. If you can convince me, I'll sell it and close down." She listened for a moment, then said, "I'll be expecting you."

She put down the phone. "Now what?"

Sally Ann sighed. "Officer Thin-gummy. Your policeman!"

Mrs. Foster called one of the bigger boys. "Tommy, go outside and see if Officer Craddock's still there. If he is, ask him if he can come in and see me for a minute. Say it's urgent."

A few minutes later a very large policeman appeared. He took off his hat, had a cup of coffee, and listened with great interest to what Mrs. Foster had to tell him.

He asked to use the phone, and then disappeared.

Things moved quickly after that.

A big black car drew up outside. Two men in dark suits got out and came up the steps and knocked at the door.

Mrs. Foster led them into the play-room.

They looked around, shaking their heads.

"It's just as I told you," said Mr. Perkins, who was tall and thin. "Rules being broken everywhere. It'd cost thousands to fix up."

Mr. Peck was short and stout.

"Thousands and thousands," he said gloomily.

Molly Morris appeared. "I understand you're from the government?"

"That's right, young lady," said Mr. Perkins.

Molly said fiercely, "Well, so am I, as it happens—from the department that runs all the day care centers around here. I've never heard of these new regulations, and I've never heard of you!"

"We're not from the town government," said Mr. Peck hurriedly. "We're from the state, you know. The capital. The state government! Way above your head, young lady."

"Oh, yes?" said Molly. "Well, maybe you'd like to show me some proper identification? And give me the name of your department head. And a phone number I can call to check up on you?"

Mr. Perkins and Mr. Peck were edging toward the door.

"It's obvious you ladies don't understand government affairs," said Mr. Peck.

"I suggest you consult your accountant," said Mr. Perkins. "He'll explain it all to you."

"We may be women, but we're not silly and helpless," said Mrs. Foster. "I think I've got the kind of accountant I need right here. You can account to him."

Officer Craddock appeared, filling up the doorway.

"Well, well, well! If it isn't Tinpot and Tring," he said cheerfully.

Mrs. Foster was amazed. "The people who wrote offering to buy my house?"

"That's right. They've tried this game before. They pretend to be from the town or the state government. They scare people into selling, then buy the place up cheap and make a quick profit. They'd have pulled this place down and sold it for a parking lot or something. We've got them now, though, thanks to you. Well done, Mrs. Foster."

Mrs. Foster smiled. "Oh, no," she said softly. "Well done, Sally Ann!"

That night in the playroom, all the toys crowded around Sally Ann to congratulate her.

"Sssplendid!" hissed Kaa. "Abssolutely ssplendid!"

"Jolly good show, old girl," rumbled Arthur the teddy bear.

And Clarence the elephant mumbled, "I suppose you did fairly well — for a doll!"

"What do you mean, for a doll?" snapped Jacko. "Sally Ann's as good as any of us — better, if you ask me!"

"That's right," said Stella proudly. "We dolls aren't silly, you know!"

"All right, all right," grumbled Clarence. "No offense!"

Albert the lion growled, "You were right and I was wrong, Sally Ann. Congratulations!"

"Three cheers for Sally Ann," said Mortimer the owl. Everyone joined in the cheers.

Even Sally Ann was a little embarrassed. "Thanks a lot," she said. "You all helped, remember. Now maybe we can get on with our real job. Playing with the children!"

About the author

After editing scripts for the *Dr. Who* television series for six years, Terrance Dicks went on to write fifty Dr. Who books based on the program. In addition he has fifty children's books to his credit, including the Goliath series.

In recent years he has worked as a script editor and producer for the BBC Classical Serial.

Mr. Dicks lives in London.

About the illustrator

Blanche Sims has illustrated many books for children, including all the titles in the Kids of the Polk Street School series by Patricia Reilly Giff and *Joey's Head* by Gladys Cretan.

Blanche Sims lives in Westport, Connecticut.